THE CASE OF THE PHANTOM FROG

By the Same Author

The Case of the Phantom Frog

A McGURK MYSTERY

By E.W. HILDICK

ILLUSTRATED BY LISL WEIL

MACMILLAN PUBLISHING CO., INC.
New York

For Andrew Bata

Macmillan Publishing Co., Inc.
866 Third Avenue, New York, N.Y. 10022
Collier Macmillan Canada, Ltd.
Printed in the United States of America

10 9 8 7 6 5 4 3 2

LIBRARY OF CONGRESS CATALOGING IN PUBLICATION DATA
Hildick, Edmund Wallace.   The case of the phantom frog.
(A McGurk mystery)   Summary: The McGurk detectives go
undercover to unmask the demon behind a phantom "werefrog" and
expose a "supernatural" hoax. [1. Mystery and detective stories] I.
Weil, Lisl. II. Title.   PZ7.H5463Cauf   [Fic]   78–10836
ISBN 0–02–743840–6

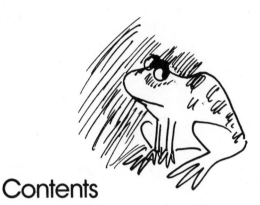

Contents

1 A Terrified Client

"I'm sorry, ma'am," said McGurk. "But we just don't *do* baby-sitting."

He spoke very firmly. His green eyes gleamed with determination as he shook his head from side to side.

"Right, men?" he said.

We all nodded: Willie Sandowsky, Wanda Grieg, Brains Bellingham, and me, Joey Rockaway. For once we were 100 percent behind our leader.

Mrs. Kranz looked disappointed.

She was sitting in the client's chair at the other end of the table in McGurk's basement—our headquarters. She was a skinny little woman with black

1

hair streaked gray. Some of the gray was hair, but from where I was sitting, next to her, I could tell there was a lot of dust mixed in. Stone dust.

"But it's so *important!*" she said.

She too had green eyes, but lighter than McGurk's and kind of bulging. I guess there must be something stubborn about people with green eyes.

"I know it's important to *you*, ma'am," said McGurk, beginning to rock slowly in his big chair at the head of the table (always a sign that he's made up his mind and isn't about to change it). "But we just don't do—"

He stopped.

Mrs. Kranz was already talking, explaining once more what her problem was.

It was certainly a tough one. I mean, there she was: an elderly widow, living alone in a big old house, minding her own business. An elderly widow who never had much time for other grownups, let alone kids, because she was always so busy with her one great interest, sculpting—carving statues and things out of great blocks of stone in her garage. Then suddenly she gets stuck with this seven-year-old boy, her nephew's son. His parents were in a hospital out on Long Island, recovering from a car crash, and it looked like they would be there another month at least.

"He's such a dear little boy," she was saying, for the second time around. "But he feels so lonely. He was born in Hungary, you know." (She said this as if it might help McGurk to change his mind— but he just kept on rocking and shaking his head as

she went on talking.) "Like me," she said. "I was
born in Hungary. And I'm the only living relative
they have over here. The only person they can trust
to look after him."

She turned to Willie.

"*You* see the problem, don't you? It was your
mother who said for me to come here and see if you
could all help me out."

Willie blushed and stroked his long nose.

"Yeah, but—"

He looked to McGurk for support, but this time
it was Wanda who took up the argument.

"It isn't that we wouldn't like to help, Mrs. Kranz,"
she said. "But you see—well—we're only kids ourselves. Most of us are only ten. And people always
get older kids to baby-sit. Like Jane Peters, who's
eighteen. They're—well—more responsible."

"But it wouldn't *be* like ordinary baby-sitting!"
said Mrs. Kranz, her eyes bulging harder. "I keep
telling you—I'll only be in the garage. If anything
goes wrong you could get hold of me immediately.
Just two hours every evening, from seven until nine,
while I catch up on my work. . . ."

She was busy on a new statue, one that she was
entering in a competition. She'd told us all about it,

even its name—*Freedom*. It was going to be her biggest yet, but all the hospital visiting had thrown her schedule way behind.

"And it must be completed by the end of the week," she had said.

Brains Bellingham coughed politely. He blinked at her through those big glasses of his and said:

"But if you're only in the garage, why bother to have baby-sitters at all, Mrs. Kranz? Couldn't you just keep stepping inside the house to—"

"Ah, no, no, no! You don't understand, little boy! When I work, I get so—so wrapped up in it—I keep forgetting where I am."

Brains too was blushing now, but with annoyance. He doesn't like being addressed as "little" any more than the rest of us—even though he *is* the youngest member, just turned nine-and-a-half. The blush was showing an angry red through the short bristly blond hair above his ears.

McGurk was frowning. His freckles were bunched together around his eyes like a dark cloud. He hates it when people suggest he's too young—no matter for what kind of job. So part of the frown was for Wanda.

He also hates it when anyone tries to take charge of an interview when he's in his big chair in his own basement. So Brains got another piece of that frown.

Willie came in for his share, too—probably because it had been his mother's recommendation that had started all this.

But McGurk's fiercest frown was for Mrs. Kranz herself, as he pointed to the notice on the basement door:

HEADQUARTERS
KEEP OUT

THE McGURK
ORGANIZATION
✳ ✳ ✳ ✳
PRIVATE INVESTIGATIONS
MYSTERIES SOLVED
PERSONS PROTECTED
MISSING PERSONS FOUND

"*That* is what we're here for, ma'am," he said, very firmly. "Assignments like that."

And *still* Mrs. Kranz wouldn't take no for an answer—which is just about the point where I decided there must be something else behind all this. I mean, Wanda had already mentioned the name of a perfectly good regular baby-sitter. So why was Mrs. Kranz being so persistent? Why *us?*

"Are you sure you can't bend the rules just this once?" she was saying. "After all, it does say 'Persons Protected' up there. And what else would this be but protecting a small person?"

McGurk's eyes narrowed a bit. I think that for a moment he too had started to suspect some other—very special—reason for Mrs. Kranz's anxiety.

"That means bodyguard duties," he said.

Mrs. Kranz sniffed. She ran a hand through her dusty hair and her eyes bulged back at McGurk almost angrily.

"And what is baby-sitting but guarding *small* bodies. Huh?"

McGurk stopped rocking. His eyes wavered. He turned to me. He always does when someone talks him into a tight corner.

"You tell the lady, Joey."

I sighed. I could still sympathize with Mrs. Kranz. But McGurk was right. Once the Organization hired itself out for that type of job, there was no telling where it might end. People would be hiring us for errands next. Or lawn-mowing. Or snow-shovelling. And who ever heard of Ellery Queen or Sherlock Holmes taking on assignments like *that?*

"Being bodyguards means—uh—moving around with the client," I said. "Protecting him or her from some real definite danger."

Mrs. Kranz's eyes bulged at me even harder, but she said nothing. McGurk nodded approval and smirked. Now that I'd gotten him out of that spot he felt that he could start doing the talking again.

"You see, Mrs. Kranz," he said, "we really are serious about this detective business. Look—we have files."

He pointed to the three boxes on the table next to my typewriter—the ones labeled: #1 MYSTERIES SOLVED, #2 LATEST MYSTERY, RECORDS AND CLUES, and #3 DETAILS OF SUSPECTS.

Then he waved airily toward Willie, sitting next to him, nearly clipping the end of the boy's nose with his knuckles.

"We have one of the best human bloodhounds in

the business here in Officer Sandowsky," he said.

He even nodded gracefully toward Wanda and me, mentioning how there was no one to beat Wanda for persistence or me for keeping accurate records. But he saved his biggest boast for Brains Bellingham.

"And this is our crime-lab expert," he said. "A scientific genius whose lab contains all the latest and most expensive equipment. We can't waste all that on *baby-sitting*."

Well, all right. Brains is very smart, scientifically. And he does have loads of instruments and charts and chemicals and electronics stuff over in his bedroom. But "latest and most expensive" equipment? Even Brains had started to squirm with embarrassment at that boast.

Mrs. Kranz, though, was very impressed. Not only that, she was encouraged. Her face brightened.

"*Expensive* equipment?" she said.

"*Very!*" said McGurk, rocking smugly.

"Well," murmured Brains, who makes most of his own equipment cheap, from old radio sets and things, "I wouldn't say—"

"*Very!*" said McGurk again, pausing in his rocking to glare at his crime-lab expert.

"So what are we arguing about?" said Mrs. Kranz.

"You need money for your crime lab. I need a baby-sitter for the next three or four nights, two hours a night, between seven and nine. How about two dollars?"

Now if there is one thing McGurk likes better than a mystery it is the chance of getting money to help solve *more* mysteries. The freckles around his eyes started squirming with indecision.

But baby-sitting. . . .

Huh-huh!

You could see the thoughts taking shape.

"Uh—I'm sorry, ma'am. But"—he sighed, then began rocking firmly—"no. I'm sorry."

"Each?" said Mrs. Kranz. "Not for two dollars *each?*"

Across the table Wanda gasped. Willie's mouth dropped open. Brains reached up to stop his glasses slipping off his nose. And McGurk froze in mid-rock, just as he'd come to the end of a swing toward Mrs. Kranz.

"*Ma'am?*" he croaked.

"That's what I said," murmured Mrs. Kranz, now sounding very confident. "Two dollars a night each. There are five of you, aren't there?" she went on, without taking her eyes off McGurk's.

"Well—yes—sure. But—"

"So that makes ten dollars a night. Just for two hours' baby-sitting."

Now that's where she went too far. She should have stopped right there at the mention of that terrific fee—the best we'd ever been offered. What she should *not* have done was mention the word "baby-sitting" again. I mean, McGurk may have his price, but he's also got his pride.

At the words "ten dollars" he looked ready to leap across the table and shake hands on the deal. At the word "baby-sitting," a kind of shudder went through him and he sat back instead.

"Well, gee, I don't know, ma'am. I mean, if the kid was in real danger—"

And that's where Mrs. Kranz made her big recovery.

"Well I can't say *that*," she murmured. "No. But —" She sighed. "All right. I'll confess. I feel like such a fool, but I guess you'd have to know sooner or later. There *is* a mystery attached to this job."

"Aha!" I thought. "Here it comes! The real, special reason, at last!"

We *all* leaned forward now. I mean, she wasn't just making this up to get our interest, we could tell.

Her face looked positively nervous, anxious—you could even say haggard. And for the first time I saw how dark the skin looked under those bulging eyes.

"Yes, ma'am?"

"Yes." She gave a shudder. "I guess everyone has something they're frightened of—more than anything else in the world. Sometimes dumb things—dumb to anyone else. . . ."

"I know what you mean, Mrs. Kranz," Wanda murmured. "With me it's rats."

"Ah, yeah!" said Willie. "Me, too! Only what I can't stand is cockroaches. Like—like I keep thinking if I'm asleep and one might crawl up my nose and—"

"All *right*, Officer Sandowsky!" said McGurk, scowling. (I guess he didn't like all this talk about his staff being scared of little things—though I could tell you of something really dumb and harmless that scares *him*, only I won't, because he'd be sure to fire me.) He turned to Mrs. Kranz. "Go on, ma'am. You were saying what scared you most."

"Sure," she said. She closed her eyes and took a deep breath. "Frogs!"

"Shut up!" McGurk growled—not at Mrs. Kranz but at Willie, who looked ready to laugh. "Shut up

or we'll discuss cockroaches!" That killed Willie's hilarity. Then, politely again, McGurk said to Mrs. Kranz: "Frogs, ma'am? You're being troubled by frogs?"

Still with her eyes closed, Mrs. Kranz nodded.

"Not just any old frogs," she muttered. "No sir! This is *some* frog. A frog that"—she gulped—"that sounds as big as a beagle pup. I—I've been hearing it croaking"—another long shudder—"ever since the child came to stay."

"Ah!" said McGurk, glancing around at the rest of us. "So you think—?"

14

"I don't know what to think," said Mrs. Kranz. "The child says he never hears it, and I must say it's usually in the evening, after he's gone to bed. I—I guess it's the time of the year or something—but I swear one's gotten into the *house*."

"But you've never actually *seen* it?" said Brains.

"No. But the sound—oh, dear—it—it's horrible!"

"Have you *looked*, Mrs. Kranz?" asked Wanda. "I mean, *carefully?*"

"Well—sure—every room—the basement—even the yard. . . ."

Wanda persisted.

"No, but if you're *that* scared, maybe you didn't go into *all* the dark corners."

Mrs. Kranz gave Wanda a look of gratitude.

"You're right, honey. You're so right. But if the McGurk Institute—"

"The McGurk *Organization*," said our leader firmly, frowning.

"If the McGurk Organization takes on the assignment, you'll be able to search properly. I—I mean *you* can get into all kinds of narrow and dirty spaces. And I—well, there are reasons why I— let's just say I don't want to call in the police or sanitation department. Oh, please—say you'll do it!"

"Of course we will, Mrs. Kranz," said Wanda.

"I might be able to fix up some frog-luring equipment," said Brains, thoughtfully.

"And I guess I could sniff it out," said Willie. "If I knew what sort of a smell to sniff *for*."

I was getting suspicious again. I was going to say, "But, *why* don't you just call in an exterminator, Mrs. Kranz?"

But McGurk was slapping the table.

"*I* make the decisions around here," he said.

Even before he went on, I knew what his answer would be. There was that look in his eyes.

"Mrs. Kranz," he said, "you've got yourself a deal. We'll take the job. You, Joey, type out the details right away. And"—his eyes gleamed brighter than ever now—"head it like this: *The Case of the Phantom Frog*."

It was that word "phantom" that had done the trick, I'm sure. McGurk's brain had latched onto something far more powerful than the words "ten dollars" or even "mystery." It was irresistible.

Anyway, that's how we came to accept our weirdest case ever.

2 The Undercover Operation

Brains was the first to raise an objection.

Just after Mrs. Kranz had left, he gave his glasses a thoughtful tug and said:

"Maybe it's a trick, all this frog stuff. Maybe she said it just to get us to go play with the kid. You heard what she said about him being lonely."

McGurk was still sitting back, glowing at the thought of a phantom to track down. It was Wanda who answered.

"I don't think it is a trick. That poor woman looked genuinely terrified."

I agreed.

"Yes. But I still think there's more to it than what

she told us. Something—well—something pretty creepy."

"Yeah!" Willie groaned. "Like a ghost. And—hey! —I bet that's why she's paying us all that money. *Danger* money!"

McGurk liked that. He suddenly rocked forward.

"Right! Right! So dangerous that we have to go in *undercover*. As baby-sitters. A *deadly dangerous undercover operation.* Yeah!"

And that was another phrase that lit him up that morning. In fact it lit us all up, including even Willie. All at once it made it seem a long, long time to 7 P.M. So we were only too glad to agree when McGurk said:

"Come on, men. Let's go there now. I want to question that kid while he's wide awake. Maybe he can give us a lead."

The Kranz house was a perfect setting for a ghost hunt. Well, maybe not as perfect as one of those old castles in a horror movie—but pretty good for our neighborhood.

It was one of those big old Spanish-looking houses. You know the sort. Rough plaster walls, peeling in places. Lots of small dark windows with real shut-

ters. Roofs with wavy red tiles and little turrets and parapets along the edges. And a wild yard with those tall, dark, narrow evergreen trees and thick dark bushes all over the place.

One tree especially interested Wanda, our climbing expert. It grew right up against the front of the house, almost hiding one of the bedroom windows.

"I'd love to have a tree like that next to our house," she said. "I'd never use the stairs. I'd climb in and out the window and use the tree every time."

Brains made one of his teacher-type clucking noises.

"Very bad for the building, a tree that close," he said. "Causes stresses. Undermines the foundations. It also causes damp and harbors bugs and moths."

"Look!" growled McGurk. "We haven't come to buy the house. We're here to solve a mystery. We're here to track down a ghost, and—"

"Hey! Yeah! And—and I think it's getting ready for us!"

That was Willie. He'd suddenly hung back. He was staring up at the tree.

"What? What is it, Willie? You smell something?"

"No. It—it—"

"Hear something?"

"No. It—" Willie was blinking. "It's just that I thought I saw something move. At the window there."

Then I saw the movement, too. A pale blur behind the screen, fading out of sight.

"That'll be the kid," said McGurk. He was already

at the door, ringing the bell, very businesslike. "Hi, Mrs. Kranz!" he said, when the door opened. "It's us. Mind if we have a talk with the kid—uh—the child—before tonight? No extra charge. It's just that we like to do these things thoroughly."

Mrs. Kranz was delighted. For the first time that day, she smiled. "Sure!" she said. "Good idea! Come on in!"

And she took us straight upstairs.

"He's still busy making himself at home," she said. "Arranging his things. Getting used to living here." She knocked, then opened the door. "Béla, you have some visitors. These are the children who're going to keep you company tonight. Isn't it nice of them?"

Big room; very small boy. Pretty gloomy dark room (it *was* the one with the tree outside); pretty gloomy dark-haired little boy.

Those were my first impressions.

The kid was looking at us as if *he* didn't think it was all that nice, having visitors.

"Hello." he said, dully.

Then he turned to the book that lay open on a desk near the window and shut it up.

"Good book?" said Wanda.

"I guess," grunted Béla.

He had a rough croaky voice for a kid of seven. It made me wonder if he'd gotten a cold or something. His skin was very pale, and his big brown eyes looked feverish.

"Why!" said Brains. "It's an encyclopedia. I have one just like it back home."

This time the kid didn't even bother to reply.

"Well," said Mrs. Kranz, looking nervous again, "I guess I'll leave you to get acquainted. Milk and cookies, anyone?"

Quick as a flash, Béla said, "No. I'm not hungry."

And he said it in such a way that poor Mrs. Kranz didn't stop to ask any of us if *we* wanted anything, as she hurried out of the room.

"This is one bratty kid!" I thought then.

"Or maybe just upset and lonely," I corrected myself, as I looked around at the room, with its dark brown furniture and its gloomy old pictures—then at the large suitcase at the side of the bed, and the stack of toys at the side of the desk.

I mean, most of those toys were brand-new: construction kits, games, things like that. And half of them hadn't been opened, still sealed inside the shiny transparent wrappers.

Wanda, Brains, and Willie were looking around and thinking pretty much the same thing, I guess, judging from the expressions on their faces. But McGurk—no. His eyes were gleaming a hard green as he sat on the edge of the bed and glared at Béla.

"This noise," he said. "You want to talk to us about it?"

Béla shrugged. He didn't shrink. Somehow he seemed to prefer McGurk's rough approach to Mrs. Kranz's gentle manner.

"Oh, *that!*" he said.

"Yeah, *that!*" said McGurk, "Mrs. Kranz says she hears it all the time. How about *you?*"

Again the shrug. And something like a sneer.

"She only *thinks* she hears it all the time. She's got frogs on the brain."

"How about *you?*" McGurk repeated—fiercer than ever.

This time the big brown eyes rolled uneasily.

"Yeah. Well. I guess I have heard a frog."

McGurk stabbed a finger at the boy.

"I'm not talking about *a* frog, sonny. I'm talking about *the* frog. The one that sounds like a giant frog."

Béla's eyes flashed.

"That's just dumb!"

"Don't you talk to me like that, kid!" growled McGurk. "We're here on official—"

"*McGurk!*" Wanda looked shocked. "The child isn't well, can't you see that? He's going through a bad time. Remember—uh—his parents. . . ."

"Yeah!" Béla's voice had gone croakier. His eyes were filling with tears. "Leave me alone. I—I'm only a kid."

"Huh!" McGurk's grunt came out gruffly and he gave us an uneasy glance. As he told us afterward, he wasn't really being cruel. He'd simply decided that if he needled the kid enough it would help to get at the truth.

It didn't seem to be working out well on Béla, that morning. He turned back to his book, pretending to ignore us completely. So McGurk tried again.

"What kind of a name *is* Béla, anyway?" he jeered. "For a *boy?* Béla's a *girl's* name!"

That stung the kid.

"It is *not!* It is a *boy's* name. My father is Hungarian. I was born in Hungary. It is a Hungarian *boy's* name."

"That's true, McGurk," I said, a bit snappishly. (I mean, his needling was beginning to bother *me* by now.) "Everyone knows that."

"Yeah!" said Willie. "Even I knew that. There's a guy on the radio. They call him Béla the Fella."

"*He* isn't a fella," said McGurk, pointing at Béla. "He's a kid."

This had gone on long enough. If McGurk kept

it up, the boy might flatly refuse to have us as
baby-sitters or playmates or whatever, and then the
whole job would be blown.

So I said the one thing that I knew would be sure
to change McGurk's attitude.

"And don't forget the guy who plays vampires
and werewolves and what-not on old horror movies.
Béla Lugosi. He was Hungarian too—I think."

McGurk's eyes widened. Old horror movies are his favorites. The gleam was replaced by a glow. A glow of respect. This time his voice was almost oily with politeness as he resumed his questioning.

"Oh—sure . . . I forgot. Say, Béla, do they really have vampires in Hungary? And werewolves. You know. In the forests there. Huh?"

But now it was Béla's turn to be rough.

"Vampires! Werewolves! Dumb, stupid kid stuff!"

"Correct!" said Brains. "There is no scientific evidence—"

"Who's asking *you?*" snarled McGurk. Then, the needler needled, he flashed back at Béla: "And who says you really are Hungarian, anyway? You talk just like anyone else. *Say* something in Hungarian."

The kid glared at McGurk. Then slowly the glare softened into a sly, gentle smile.

"All right," he said huskily. Then, hesitating a lot, but still with the smile, he said something that *sounded* genuine, anyway. Something swishy at first, which then became clacky, like metal, and ended with a soft bark.

Long after the case was wrapped up, I got Mrs. Kranz to write down what Béla said that morning, and here it is:

```
SOSE FOGOD
MEGTALÁLNI AZTA
BÉKÁT
```

"Well?" said McGurk, turning to me. "*Was* it Hungarian?"

"How should I know?"

"You're the word expert, aren't you?"

"Only American words."

He gave me a look of disgust, then turned to Béla. "What's it mean?"

The sly smile spread wider.

"You'll find out!"

And that was all we got from Béla on that visit.

"We'll have to watch him closely, men," said McGurk, on our way back. "That kid's got a very old look about him. I think he could have told us much more than he did."

"Yes," agreed Brains. "I wouldn't put it past him to be doing it himself."

"Doing what himself?" asked Willie.

"Making frog noises. Just to scare Mrs. Kranz. Knowing how she hates them."

"Oh, come *on!*" said Wanda. "He's just a poor frightened little boy. Can't you see that? In fact— well—you know what I thought that look in his eyes was, most of the time?"

"What?"

Wanda lowered her voice.

"A *haunted* look," she said. "Definitely haunted. Like something scares the daylights out of him, too."

That silenced us all for a while.

Then McGurk gave a satisfied grunt.

"Maybe you're right. But we'll soon see. Don't forget we'll be at the scene ourselves, between seven and nine tonight. No one's going to fool *us!*"

3 The Voice of the Frog

I have to say this much for Béla: He was a much better baby-sit*tee* than any of us had ever been. The moment Mrs. Kranz left us alone with him up in his room, just after seven that evening, he did *not*:

leap out of bed and say, "O.K., let's play hide-and-go-seek out in the yard!" or holler out for hot dogs, or chocolate ice cream, or any other forbidden bedtime food; or insist on watching TV or playing records; or demand some dumb bedtime story to be repeated over and over again until *everyone* fell asleep.

No. He simply lay back on his pillows, closed his eyes, and said:

"O.K. You can leave me now. I feel very tired. Just don't turn off the light. I—I—"

Here his eyelids fluttered open and the brown eyes turned nervously from side to side.

"That's all right, Béla," said Wanda, gently. "I guess we were all scared of the dark at one time or another."

His eyes opened wider. For a second or two they flashed angrily. Then he closed them, gave that sly smile, and said:

"It isn't that I'm scared. It's just that this is a strange room to me, and I like to know where everything is if I have to go to the bathroom."

"Sure!" said McGurk, a bit impatiently. (We had a plan all ready, and he wanted to get down to putting it into operation.) "We understand. But if you hear anything—uh!—I mean *need* anything, just holler. O.K.?"

Béla nodded. His eyes were still closed. His breathing was beginning to sound deep and regular.

We started to tiptoe out.

"Just one thing," he said, as we reached the door.

"Oh-oh! Here we go!" I thought. "He's like the

rest of them, after all. Is it going to be ice cream and Coke? Or some stupid game where he'll throw a temper tantrum if we don't let him win?"

But it wasn't anything like that.

"Wanda," he said, "is the window open? It's a warm night and it gets kind of stuffy in here."

Wanda went across and checked.

"It's open a little at the bottom," she said. "Would you like me to open it at the top also?"

"No! No!" He raised his head sharply. "No. The bottom's fine. It gets too drafty with the top open as well. Oh—and while you're over there, would you please turn the lampshade so I don't get the glare in my eyes?"

The lamp was on the desk near the window. Wanda turned the shade so that the brightest light was shining away from the bed and through the window and screen, onto the dark leaves of the tree.

"You sure you wouldn't like your pillows plumped?" said McGurk, with a sarcastic twist to his mouth. He was getting *very* impatient by now. "Or your temperature checked? Or—"

"Thank you, Wanda," said Béla, sleepily. "That's just fine. Good night, everybody."

We murmured our good-nights and finally left him. Everything seemed peaceful. The only sound was the faint *chink! chink!* of Mrs. Kranz's hammer from out in the garage.

"Right!" said McGurk, when we'd got back down to the living room. "Now we can proceed with our plan. Willie—get away from that TV—we're here on official business. Brains, just run through the plan one more time, will you?"

Brains nodded eagerly and adjusted his glasses.

McGurk had referred to *our* plan, I know. But this was really Brains's idea—and a very scientific one at that.

"We're here to locate a noise, right?"

We nodded.

"Or a ghost," Willie added.

"Baloney," said Brains. "No such things. It is either a frog or a fraud or a freak."

"A freak?" said McGurk, looking startled. This was a new one to him, as well as to the rest of us. "How do you mean—a freak?" he asked, beginning to look at Brains suspiciously.

"A plumbing freak," said Brains. "It occurred to me up there, when Béla mentioned the bathroom. It could be one of those freak noises the plumbing makes at times."

We must all have been looking a bit disappointed at that. I mean, it was nearly as bad as a straight baby-sitting job, getting a high-powered detective organization to deal with a blocked *drain,* for heaven's sake!

Brains must have sensed this, because he hurried on.

"But whatever it is—frog, fraud, phantom, or freak—its chief characteristic is a *sound.* Right?"

We nodded.

"Right," said Brains.
"Well, I've done quite a bit
of research into sonics and—"

"What-ics?" said Willie.

"Sonics. The science of
sounds. And one thing is
very clear. Sounds are very
difficult to get a bearing on
with the naked ear. Directionwise."

"He means you can't be sure where they're coming from," I said, seeing the glassy look come into Willie's eyes again. "Sure," I said, "we all know that, Brains. It's the way ventriloquists work. So?"

"So it's no use us all sitting here in one place, waiting for the noise. We'd never be sure just where it was coming from."

"Right," said McGurk. "So the plan. Get to the plan."

His eyes were flitting about uneasily, as if he expected the noise to sound off at any minute, before we were ready.

"So the plan is to disperse ourselves intelligently around the house. And wait. And listen. And as soon as we hear the sound, check with each other on the *general* direction. That way we should be able to pinpoint it."

"Great!" said McGurk, taking over from there. "So here's what we do."

He may not have known enough science to think of the original idea, but when it came to organizing there was no one to beat McGurk. I mean, we'd only been in the house twice, both for very short times at that, but he had it all cased out. Just take a look at these rough plans of the first and second floors of the Kranz house, and you'll see what I mean.

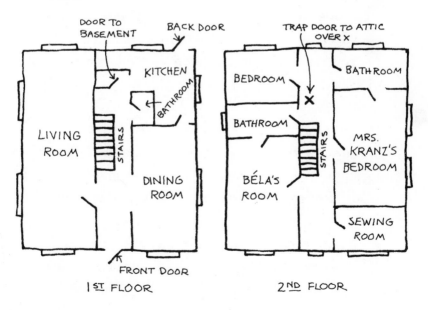

As I said, these are *very* rough sketches, but they show all that we needed to know. And here's how McGurk arranged the Frog Watch:

"First," he said, "we have all doors to every room open—except Béla's. That way the sound can have a free passage. Right, Brains?"

Brains nodded.

"Yes. And the trap door to—"

"I know! I know! I'm getting to that. In fact I'll deal with that one first. On the landing upstairs, between the back rooms, there's a trap door leading to the attic. You, Wanda, will get up there—there's a stepladder in the kitchen—and you'll open that trap door and you'll perch on the edge. Got that?"

"You bet!" said Wanda, her eyes shining at being given a job after her own heart.

"Brains, you will stand *on* the landing, between the open door of Mrs. Kranz's bedroom and—"

"Sure," said Brains. "And don't worry. I will keep turning slowly, through a full 360-degree circle, ready to catch the direction, whether it comes from—"

"Right! Right! So long as you don't get dizzy. Now—to cover the downstairs area—which I think is the most likely—there'll be me, Joey, and Willie.

Willie—I want you to cover the basement."

"Huh?" Willie gave a little yelp. His face was turning pale already. "But—"

"I know. You're afraid of roaches, right? So no sweat. All I want you to do is stand at the top of the basement steps, with the door open, listening in case the sound comes from down there. That O.K.?"

Willie nodded, with a look of great relief.

Then McGurk gave me the door between the kitchen and dining room to cover, and himself the foot of the stairs near the open door of the living room, and we all went to our posts.

The result?

Better than *I* expected, anyway.

I mean, after the first half-hour, when we'd stopped raising false alarms over ordinary noises— like the refrigerator starting to hum, and a cat squawling outside, and Mrs. Kranz using a heavier hammer on her statue, and a dripping tap, and a creaking board, and Wanda fidgeting on the edge of the trap door because she kept brushing spider webs out of her hair, and Willie's nose starting to wheeze and whistle in his excitement—it began to seem very quiet indeed. *Unnaturally* quiet, as if some strange creature had started to wake, and stir

out of its lair. Spooky, I guess, is the word that best describes it. Totally spooky.

Then:

"*QUAAAAARK!*"

We heard it.

Except if you just made the sound the way I've had to write it, you'd have no true idea.

Because believe me, this was no ordinary sound.

"*Shnnaquaaaarark!*"

That's more like it. Long, drawn-out. Rasping. High-pitched. A bit like a snore, maybe—but much more like a snarl.

"*Shushnaquaaaraaaarnaaaragraaark!*"

The snarl of an angry monster that had just been aroused from a deep, deep sleep.

4 A Locked-Room Mystery?

There was a pause. A hush. Followed by mutterings and whisperings from every part of the house.

"Joey!" McGurk whispered, sticking his head around the corner of the dining-room door. "Where d'you think it came from?"

"Not in here," I said. "Not from the kitchen, either."

"Right! Follow me. . . . Willie—how about the basement?"

"No—no way. Not from down there. No, sir!"

"O.K. That rules out the first floor. Because it sure didn't come from the living room or the hallway. . . . Come on, men. Let's see what the others can tell us."

Wanda was already climbing down from the attic when we reached the top of the stairs.

"Definitely from someplace below *me*," she said.

Which left Brains.

The originator of the plan.

I guess he must have been under greater stress than any of us others—wanting his plan to be a success. Or maybe it was because he'd been slowly turning around and around all this time and it *had* made him a little dizzy.

Whatever it was, it seemed to have struck him dumb for the time being. And rigid.

He was standing stiffly at attention, his eyes shut, with every bristle on his head seeming to stand at attention, too.

"Brains!" whispered McGurk. "You all right?"

Brains gave a little shiver, then opened his eyes.

And they were gleaming as brightly as McGurk's had ever done.

"I stopped dead," he murmured excitedly. "The second I heard it. Just like this—with my right ear toward the open door of Mrs. Kranz's room and my left ear toward Béla's closed door."

"Well? Go *on* then!"

McGurk looked ready to shake him until his glasses flew off.

"Well, allowing for the difference in the quality of sound through an open door and a closed door, I don't think there's any doubt about it." Brains jerked his head toward the closed door. "It came from in there."

"Right!" growled McGurk. "That's just what I expected."

And without further hesitation he stepped over to Béla's room, jerked open the door, and switched on the light.

Then he stood glaring around the room, with the rest of us crowded behind him.

A gentle sound came from the bed. Not a croak, not a snarl, not even a snore. Just the heavy breathing of a sleeping child.

Or a *seemingly* sleeping child.

"Careful you don't wake him," said Wanda, as McGurk went prowling around the room.

"Forget *him!*" said McGurk. "Search! All the corners. Behind the desk there. The bed itself if we have to. Everywhere a frog could have leaped or hopped or run or crawled."

As we went about doing all this, the sound of heavy breathing continued to come from the bed. Even Wanda had to agree that there was something phony about it, after a while.

"He's only pretending," she said, bending over Béla. "Look. See the way his eyes are squeezed tight."

"Yeah!" growled McGurk. "And how about that grin on his face? Hey, you!" He gave Béla a rough poke in the chest. "Quit acting. I want to talk to you."

Slowly, Béla's eyelids relaxed and began to open.

"Oh, hello, Aunty Kranz!" he murmured, in a sleepy voice. "Is it morning already?"

McGurk looked as if he could have hauled the kid out of bed for that Aunty Kranz crack. But he's nothing if not professional when he's on a case.

"All right," he said, calmly enough. "Did you hear it?"

"Hear what?" asked Béla.

"You know what. The frog noise, sonny. The frog noise."

"The frog noise? Now you really *do* sound like Aunty Kranz."

"Grr! Move aside!"

And—good as his word—McGurk pulled off the covers and began to search the bed.

Well, it was the only place left as far as I could see. We'd searched every corner of that room pretty thoroughly. We'd even looked into the clothes closet because the door had been left open a crack and a frog could have gotten in there. I glanced around the room again just to make sure—but no. Apart from us kids, the only living creatures in that room were a couple of moths, flying around the lamp—and there was no way *they* could have made such a noise.

Sure, there was the door leading from Béla's room into the bathroom, but it was firmly closed. And if the frog—or Béla—had been in there, Brains would have been sure to hear it through the *open* door leading to the landing. So, what with that and the fact that the window was closed, it was beginning to look like one of those great Locked-Room mysteries—the toughest of all to solve—where nothing and no one can get out or get in.

Then it hit me.

"Hey! Wait a minute!" I said, as McGurk tossed the covers back into place over the still smirking Béla. "What about—?"

McGurk turned quickly and gave me a warning frown.

"Later," he said. "We'll discuss this later. In private." Then he turned back to Béla and forced a sickly grin to his face. "Sorry about this, son," he said. "Our mistake. The sound must have come from someplace else. But we were only doing our duty."

"Sure," said Béla, putting on his sleepy act again. "That's O.K. Don't forget to leave the light on when you go out."

This brought a gasp from Wanda, but McGurk shushed her the way he'd shushed me. And it wasn't until we were back downstairs that he spoke up.

"Well that's one thing we learned for sure, men.

Frog or no frog, fraud or no fraud, Béla is up to no good."

"Uh—how d'you figure that, McGurk?" asked Willie. "*I* didn't—"

"Because of the—" both Wanda and I began to say together.

"Yeah! The light," said McGurk. "When we left him just after seven it was *on*. He especially asked for it to be left on. But when we went in after the noise, the room was all dark. Which means only one thing, right?"

"The—the *frog* turned it off?"

"*No*, Willie! The kid himself. For some reason, he must have got up and switched it off."

We nodded. Even Willie was starting to get the picture.

"Yeah—but why?" he asked. "I thought he said he *needed* the light."

McGurk grunted.

"When we know the answer to that we'll have solved the mystery," he said. "Any ideas?"

We looked at each other.

Not even Brains seemed to have an answer ready.

I frowned.

"Joey?" said McGurk. "You got a theory?"

Slowly, I shook my head.

"Sorry," I said. "I was thinking of something else. Something else that wasn't the same as when we left him."

"You mean the window?" said Wanda. "Yes. I noticed that, too. I even searched there, between the window and the screen, but no frog. So I guess that whatever Béla got up to do in the darkness— maybe go to the door to hear what we were saying —he found the draft too much for him."

"Maybe," said McGurk, thoughtfully. "Maybe.

. . . Anyway, the frog noises seem to have stopped for tonight."

"So what do we do next?" asked Wanda. "Go back to our posts just to make sure?"

McGurk looked uncertain. He was still puzzling over the problem of the light, I could tell. Wanda's theory had sounded reasonable enough to me, but it obviously hadn't satisfied him.

So while McGurk frowned and doubtfully shook his head, it was left to Brains to suggest the next move.

"Forget about the Frog-Watch posts," he said. "We know now where the source of the sound is. What we have to do is fix up an even more scientific method of tracking it down tomorrow night."

McGurk looked up sharply.

"And what would that be?" he said.

"Leave it to me," said Brains. "I've already got an idea. Just give me time to whip it into shape." He grinned around at us confidently. "You'll see," he said. "By tomorrow night at this time we'll have that Phantom Frog on toast."

"I'd rather have *sardines* on toast!" muttered Willie, giving a little shudder.

5 The Frog Appears

When we took up our duties the second night, we were much better equipped. We knew now the general area the frog noise was coming from and we also had a prime suspect. In line with all this, Brains had been very busy making his preparations—and so had McGurk and I.

"Mrs. Kranz," said McGurk, just as she was getting ready to go out to the garage, "you did say we could search everywhere, didn't you?"

"I certainly did! That's the whole idea of it."

"Well, ma'am, in that case, we need to cover ourselves. Sign this, please."

51

Mrs. Kranz's eyes popped as she stared down at the folded sheet of paper that McGurk had had me specially prepare. This is what it looked like on the outside:

The fancy bits were just regular sevens typed over eights. I was very proud of them. But of course it wasn't admiration for my typing that had made Mrs. Kranz's eyes pop.

"Search warrant?" she said.

"Yes," said McGurk. "All detectives need them in cases like this. Open it, please, and sign where it says."

"Well, sure—it's hardly necessary, but—sure. I'm glad to see you're still being so thorough."

So here it is. Our first search warrant. Signed by Mrs. Kranz.

```
Be it known by these presents that
        Officer Jack P. McGurk
          and any or all other
      officers of his Organization

are hereby authorized to search the premises of
Mrs. G. Kranz in all rooms, outbuildings, and
yard thereof, including furnishings, fixtures,
fittings, chests, boxes, and other receptacles
therein, and to do this without restriction or
hindrance.      Signed .G..Kranz...........
                           G. Kranz (Mrs.)
```

"O.K.," said McGurk, tucking it away in his pocket and looking very pleased with himself, after Mrs. Kranz had gone. "So now we're all set for *your* idea, Brains."

"Sure," said Brains. He was already opening the box he'd brought along. "Why don't we get it fixed up right away?"

His idea was simple. All it required was a microphone, a long piece of wire, and a small amplifier with a loudspeaker.

"We'll set the microphone up in Béla's bedroom," he explained once more, as we went upstairs. "Then we run the lead down to the amplifier and loudspeaker, which we leave in the living room. That way we can sit in comfort while we wait for the frog or whatever it is to sound off."

"But what if Béla spots the microphone?" said Wanda, as we paused on the landing.

"Oh, he'll spot it!" said Brains. "We're not going to hide it or anything. In fact, we're going to tell him what we're doing. Right, McGurk?"

"Right!" said McGurk, his eyes gleaming.

"But supposing he's the one who's been making the noises," said Wanda. "It'll warn him off."

"Right again!" said McGurk. "Then, if there's complete silence tonight, we'll know for sure."

"He could sabotage it, even," said Brains. "Pull the wires out. Then we'd also know for sure."

"But my guess is that he'll try something cute," McGurk said grimly. "I have a feeling about that kid. . . . Anyway, let's get it set up."

Béla was pretty cool, I have to admit. He didn't seem to be paying much attention as Brains busied himself with the apparatus—fixing the microphone on the desk and running the wires down under the rug and out onto the landing.

"Now this isn't going to disturb you," said Wanda. "Just pretend it isn't there."

"It's just that you're such a heavy sleeper," said McGurk, with a touch of sarcasm. "So if the phantom frog does pay you a visit again, and you go on sleeping like last night, it won't matter. *We'll* hear it."

"You got frogs on the brain!" was all Béla said, wearily closing his eyes and turning onto his side. "Don't forget to leave the light on when you're through."

"That is one strange little boy," said Wanda, when we were back in the living room and Brains was fussing with the volume of the loudspeaker. "I get

the feeling he knows a whole lot more about everything than he admits to."

"Yes, well," said McGurk, "he's met his match
now, anyway. Because even if he's a genius, he can't
know more than us five combined. . . . O.K., Willie.
Switch on the TV. Just keep the sound down is all."

We were especially glad about Brains's idea because that night there was a "Peanuts" special and
we didn't want to miss any of it if we could help it.
Even so, we were a bit more interested at first in
putting our ears close to Brains's loudspeaker—won-
dering if it would work all right. But after a while,
when Brains told us the hissing noise proved we
were in full radio contact with Béla's room and that
he'd let us know if more interesting sounds came
through, we settled to watch the program.

And for the next half-hour or so we could have
been *real* baby-sitters, eating candy and laughing
and murmuring at a good TV show. In fact, we became so much like regular baby-sitters we even forgot about the baby we were supposed to be sitting.
Especially when Snoopy got into a bind with—

But that's where the loudspeaker burst into life.
Our loudspeaker, not the TV's.

"Shushnaquaaaraaaanaaaragraaark!"

The rasping, snoring, snarling sound cut right through the TV sound and had us all sitting up rigid in our seats.

"It—gosh—it sounds bigger than ever!" gasped Wanda.

"It sounds like it stepped right up to the microphone," whispered Brains, looking very shocked.

"It sounds like it *swallowed* the microphone!" moaned Willie.

Then:

"What are we waiting for, men? Come on!"

McGurk was already heading for the stairs.

We followed.

Behind us, there came another squawk from the loudspeaker, and another, and another, each more horrible than the last, each one acting like a brake and slowing us down on our way to the room where the sound was really coming from.

Even McGurk hesitated at the door. His freckles were standing out against the whiteness of his skin.

Then he took a big breath, said, "Right! Keep your eyes peeled!"—and threw open the door.

Well . . . this time the light was still on.

And this time there was no need to go searching for the frog.

It was there, all right.

Plumb in the middle of the pillow on Béla's bed.

A big frog as frogs go, but not as huge as it had sounded.

In fact it looked a sort of *nice* frog, in spite of the warts—with a pale browny-greeny skin and large liquid brown eyes edged with gold.

"He's *cute!*" said Wanda, stepping forward for a closer look. The frog throbbed a little under his chin. "Look at those lovely eyes. They're just like Béla's."

"Yes," said Brains. "But where *is* Béla?"

We glanced around.

No sign of the kid.

Then, in a harsh whisper, McGurk said something
that made me come out in goose bumps all over.

"Yeah!" he said. "Where *is* Béla? Stand back,
Wanda. Stand back, the rest of you. This could be
dangerous."

"Huh?" Willie was already backing to the door.
"Wh-why?"

"The kid comes from Hungary, right? Where
they have werewolves—people who change into
wolves."

"S-so?"

Wanda had started backing away now.

"So," McGurk went on, looking grimmer than
ever, "what we might have here, men, is a case of
a—a were*frog!*"

That was enough for Willie.

And when, at the word "werefrog," the creature
on the pillow looked up, and something like a bub-
ble of gum swelled up under its mouth, and it
came out with a long, leering, knowing, rasping
snarl, it was enough for the rest of us—McGurk in-
cluded.

We ran. We ran downstairs and into the living
room and didn't take a breath until the door was
firmly shut behind us.

6 The Trance

Brains was the first to speak.

"I—I still can't believe it. It's impossible!"

"Me either!" I said. "These things just don't happen in real life!"

McGurk grunted. He was standing in front of the living-room door, staring down at the handle as if he expected to see it slowly turn any minute.

"That's what the victims in werewolf movies always say," he muttered. "Impossible. Just before it sinks its fangs into them."

Willie looked rapidly from side to side.

"Where's the phone? Maybe we'd better call the police. Or—or get Mrs. Kranz to come in."

"And make ourselves look like idiots?" said Brains.

Wanda gave a kind of shivering sigh.

"It was no ordinary frog, anyway. I've never seen one quite like it. And did you notice its feet? The way they—"

"Just because it isn't an *ordinary* frog doesn't mean it's a werefrog," said Brains. "Do you realize how many varieties of frogs there are? Heck—in that collection of stuffed frogs they had at the Town Museum there were over fifty different kinds. And that was from the United States alone."

McGurk turned to him. The color had started to come back to his face. His eyes glinted angrily.

"So all right then, Professor Bellingham! If you're so sure this isn't a werefrog, why don't you go up and capture it? Huh?"

Brains backed off then. He may be super-intelligent, but he's still younger and smaller than the rest of us. He started to fiddle about with the controls of his amplifier and loudspeaker—now quite dead, by the way.

"Well—I mean—I—I'm not saying it might not be *dangerous*. A—a poisonous toad, maybe. Or—or—"

"Or a poisonous *werefrog*, huh?"

Brains took ahold of himself. He looked up defiantly.

"Anyway, surely the thing to do next is look for Béla. He must be somewhere in the house."

"Yeah!" said Willie. "Right there on that pillow. Shaped like a frog."

Brains ignored that. He was sounding much more confident as he continued:

"And when we find him, and then look in on the frog, and see them both together—maybe *then* you'll all be convinced I'm right."

McGurk nodded. I guess he could see the leadership slipping away if he didn't make an effort.

"Fair enough," he said. "We—we'll start with the bathroom, the one next to *his* room. Then the other rooms up there. . . . But I still have a terrible feeling we'll be wasting our time."

I had to admire McGurk then. He was scared, all right. Just as scared as Willie or Wanda or me. Or even Brains—because for all his scientific talk, our crime-lab expert wasn't the first to go back up those stairs. Oh, no! He hung back with the rest of us and it was left to McGurk to take the lead. Pale, tight-lipped, tense, clutching a bunch of garlic cloves he'd grabbed from the kitchen: that was Mc-

Gurk. Doing his duty as Head of the Organization.

(The garlic cloves were the only things he could think of that might be protection against a werefrog. I tried to tell him that it was only supposed to work against vampires, but he said we had to use what was there and hope for the best.)

But he was right about wasting our time. We searched Béla's bathroom first, going in through the landing door. No Béla. We then searched each of the other rooms up there—except for Béla's bedroom. We searched them in turn, leaving Brains on the landing (he volunteered) to make sure Béla didn't sneak out of any of the extra doors. No Béla in any of *those* rooms, either.

Which left only his own room.

"All right, Brains," said McGurk, looking pale again. "This was your idea. You don't believe in werefrogs. So you lead the way."

Brains tried to produce a confident smile, a real "cheese" smile, but it started crumbling at the edges. He took up the challenge, though.

"Sure," he mumbled. And slowly, cautiously, he opened the door and peered in.

Then he relaxed.

"It's O.K.," he said. "The frog's gone. It's Béla again."

He was right. The boy was back in bed, his eyes tight shut, and a big blissful smile on his face.

"He's changed back!" whispered Willie, with so much awe in his voice that it stopped us in our tracks.

Even Brains lost some of his cool then, and it was left to McGurk to take over the lead again and step up to the bed.

"Béla!" he murmured, very respectfully, holding out the garlic with both hands clasped together, like it was a .38 police special he was training on the kid.

No response.

"Hey, Béla! Quit fooling. Tell us what happened."

Still no response. The eyes stayed closed, the smile stayed fixed. The kid lay there rigid, and I do believe we could have stuck pins into him and he still wouldn't have moved. I was beginning to learn about Béla.

"He—he looks like he's in a trance," Wanda whispered.

McGurk nodded—still very tense.

"That would figure. They always do."

"Do—do what, McGurk?"

"Go into a trance when they change back!"

Brains gave his teacher-type cluck.

"Aw, use your heads!" he groaned. "Let's look for the frog. Like I said before—if we find it, maybe that'll convince you there's been no changing."

The figure on the bed remained perfectly still, but I could swear the smile had broadened a bit.

"Only this time let's look in the drawers and that suitcase," Brains went on. "After all, we do have a search warrant now. That's what you got Mrs. Kranz to sign it for, isn't it, McGurk?"

The reminder about the search warrant seemed to pull McGurk back closer to his usual self.

"Yeah, sure," he murmured, taking out the folded paper. "Only—how do you show it to the suspect if he's in a trance?"

Brains clucked again.

"If he really is a werefrog he'll see it with his eyes shut," he said sarcastically. "Here, let me." He took the warrant and held it up in front of the boy's face. Béla remained rigid, smiling, seemingly sleeping and dreaming about a banquet of live flies and moths and other yummy frog food. This annoyed Brains. "Listen, you!" he growled. "This is a search warrant, signed by Mrs. Kranz. We're going to search through your drawers and things."

I watched *very* closely then—but Béla just didn't move a muscle.

McGurk was getting more like his usual self every second.

"Right!" he said, in his old businesslike, bossy way. "Joey and Brains—you look in those drawers over there. Wanda—you go through that pile of toys and games. Willie—" Suddenly McGurk's eyes widened. "Hey, yes! I'd been forgetting. Can you *sniff* it out, Willie?"

Willie shrugged.

"Well, sure. Like I said before. If I knew what a frog smelled like. And—and you put that garlic back in your pocket."

"A kind of damp smell, I imagine," said Brains, over his shoulder, as he looked up from a drawerful of undershirts. "An *outdoorsy* damp smell, if you know what I mean."

Willie groaned and began to look scared again.

"Oh, no! Not a *swampy* smell?"

"Yes," said Brains. "Exactly."

"Well—" Willie gulped and pointed a trembling finger at the boy in the bed. "Well that I *do* get a whiff of. From *him*. Even through the garlic." Then he lowered his nose and his finger and, trembling more than ever, said: "And it's even stronger from that case down there."

"Well, that's where the frog must *be*, then!" said Brains eagerly, going across to the suitcase. "Where else?"

And even as he spoke, he was snapping open the catches.

I kept my eyes on Béla. "This should make him jump up," I was thinking. "If Brains is right."

But there was still no movement.

Then I heard Willie gasp and I looked down.

They hadn't found the frog. The case was empty. Empty, that is, apart from a large, damp, yellowish-gray stain on the bottom.

"See that!" McGurk whispered. "I—I bet he sleeps in there with the lid on during daylight hours. Like—like Dracula in his coffin!"

Then there was a movement from the boy on the bed. Still smiling, still with his eyes tight shut, his top lip lifted a little, his throat began to quiver just under the chin, and: *"Shquaaark!"* he went— just like the frog, but not so long or loud.

This time we didn't run. But we *backed* out every step of the way from that room. And when we got back downstairs, no one spoke for at least five minutes.

What the others were thinking, I don't know. Nothing very pleasant, that's for sure. Not even Brains, who'd taken off his glasses and was polishing them hard with the edge of his shirt. Now that he'd gotten over his early shock he wasn't acting terrified, exactly, but he was thinking hard and he seemed troubled.

As for me, for all my doubts, McGurk's and Willie's fear must have been catching. For now I was remembering something else. Those Hungarian words the boy had hissed and clacked and barked at McGurk on our first meeting with him.

Could they have been an ancient curse?

The Curse of the Werefrogs, maybe?

7 The Lie-Detector Test

We didn't say anything about all this to Mrs. Kranz when she came in all covered in white dust, just after nine, and Mrs. Sandowsky drew up in the car to take us home. I mean, how do you tell someone that you suspect her nephew's only child of being a werefrog? Especially someone who's scared stiff of ordinary frogs anyway. It would have been enough to give her a heart attack.

So McGurk just told her we were working on "a certain angle" and would let her know as soon as we had something solid. Then we went home—subdued, perplexed, and still feeling spooked.

We all had a pretty bad night's sleep, I'm sure. I

know I did, dreaming that McGurk himself kept changing into a speckled green toad. And when we met in McGurk's basement the next morning, Willie told us he'd been having nightmares, too; and Wanda had dark shadows under her eyes. Even Brains looked tired—though for a different reason.

"I lay awake half the night," he said. "I read up all I could find about werewolves and things. And I *still* can't buy it," he said, staring defiantly into McGurk's weary, uneasy eyes.

"So?" growled McGurk.

"So there's only one thing *to* think. That kid's been making fools of us. I mean, I'm an expert at making fools of people, don't forget. I'm the guy who invented the Invisible Dog."

McGurk began to look interested.

"Yeah. I said all along that Béla's a tricky character. And very slippery. But how do we prove it? How do we wrap up the case and earn our fee? I mean, where does the frog come from? Where does he hide it?"

Brains was smiling now.

"That's just what I've been working on ever since breakfast," he said. "I think we ought to question him closely."

McGurk groaned.

"What good would *that* do? How will we ever get the truth out of *him?* How will we know whether he's telling lies or—"

"*Here's* how!" said Brains, all flushed.

He'd been sitting at the table with an old flat cardboard box on his knees. Now he brought it up, placed it on the table, and whipped off the lid.

Wires: red and green and yellow. Neat little spring terminals clamping the wires in place. A meter. A control knob. Some small batteries.

That's all we saw at first.

Then Brains said the magic words that made it suddenly seem like a gift from heaven.

"A lie detector!"

I remembered how he'd promised to make us one the day he joined the Organization. Since then, we'd been so busy on other things that I'd forgotten all about it.

McGurk's eyes were shining.

"No kidding?"

"No kidding," said Brains.

"And it really works?"

"It really works."

"How?"

Brains showed us two wires with loose bare ends.

"You take one in one hand and the other in the other and look—" The needle had flickered and moved to the middle of the scale. "The circuit's completed. A very small current of electricity is going through my body."

"Does—does it hurt?" asked Willie.

"No. Too small. But the reason it flows at all is because my hands—everybody's hands—are very slightly damp with sweat. And when they get excited, more sweat comes—" He took his hands off the wires and licked his fingers. "Like this. And—" *Click!* He'd gripped the wires again and this time the needle shot right to the end of the scale. "It registers."

"But what's that got to do with lying?" Wanda asked.

"Everything," said Brains. "Because when you lie, even if you keep a straight face, you get a little nervous, a little excited, and more sweat comes, and the needle flicks."

"Try it on me!" said McGurk.

Well, that was a riot. I mean, it looked as if McGurk was lying even before he'd opened his mouth. As soon as he touched the wires the needle flashed to the right and bounced off the end of the scale.

Brains hurriedly switched off. "That's because you're excited, McGurk. Just plain excited. For you, I'd have to load the circuit a bit more."

He switched some of the wires around, and this time when McGurk got hold of the end pieces, the meter needle went only to the halfway mark.

"Now ask!" said McGurk.

"O.K. . . . Do you really want to solve this case?"

"No!" said McGurk, grinning.

And the needle flashed to the end of the scale.

"*That* was a lie," said Brains.

"And how!" said McGurk, gleefully. "Why don't we use it on Béla *now*, right away?"

But Brains wasn't having any over-eagerness spoil his scientific preparations.

"No," he said. "Let's give it a thorough testing first. Willie?"

Willie backed off.

"No!" he said. "No way! I—I've got a very sensitive skin. That's what gives me such a keen sense of smell. *I'd* get a shock even if you guys wouldn't!"

"It's only a nine-volt battery, you dummy!"

"I don't care. I—"

"Here. Let me try," said Wanda.

She proved to be the opposite to McGurk. Very cool. Very dry. At first I thought the circuit had broken down, because when she gripped the wires the needle stayed at zero.

"This is the best type of subject," said Brains, rearranging the wires to get a center reading. "Because when the needle flickers with *them*, you know they really are lying and it isn't just excitement or general nervousness. I only hope Béla's the same."

Well, Wanda kept that needle steady for four or five routine questions—like what day it was, and how old she was last birthday—which she answered truthfully. But when McGurk shot at her this question:

"Do you ever think you could run this organization better than me?"

—and she answered:

"No! Never!"

—the needle flicked and she had to admit she had lied.

That was enough for McGurk. He told me I could have a turn later, but right now the detector was required for serious business: Béla the Werefrog.

"Bring him in for questioning," he said. "Now! You go get him, Wanda. He seems to trust you more than the rest of us."

"What if he's asleep in the suitcase?" said Willie. "You know—like Dracula."

But there was no need to worry. We'd only had time to work out a few questions before Wanda was back with the kid.

Here are those questions, just as I wrote them down:

LIE DETECTOR INTERROGATION
SUBJECT: BÉLA EGRI

1. What is your name?
2. Where are you staying?
3. Are you really a werefrog?
4. (If answer to #3 is YES) But didn't you say there were no such things as werewolves and vampires?

Béla had that sly grin on his face again. He also had a curious look in his eyes as he glanced around the basement.

"Detectives, huh? Some detectives!"

But then he backed off almost as violently as Willie when McGurk shoved the lie detector toward him.

"What is this?"

"A lie detector."

"You going to torture me with it?"

"No!" Smiling patiently, Brains explained the way it worked in even simpler terms than he'd used with us. "O.K.?"

Béla still looked doubtful. But the grin was beginning to return.

"You do it first," he said to McGurk.

"Sure!" said McGurk, grabbing the wires and causing the needle to jerk already and Brains to cluck and start rearranging the circuit again. Then, when the needle was fairly steady, Brains asked McGurk some routine questions, and when McGurk lied about what day it was and the needle kicked, Brains turned to Béla and said: "See? He said it was Sunday when it's really Wednesday. So the needle jumped."

Béla nodded. The grin was back in full force now.

"Can I ask him a question?"

"Sure!" said McGurk. "Go ahead."

"Are you as dumb as you look?"

"*No!*" roared McGurk, and the needle shot up. "I mean *yes!* I mean—argh!—what kind of a question is *that?*"

It was a perfect example of an *excited* response without any lying.

But Béla was ready. He took the bare wires firmly in his fingers and there was hardly a reading. I mean, it was really dead. If he wasn't a frog, he was certainly as cold-blooded as one.

"Beautiful!" Brains gloated, fixing the wires to get a better reading. "A perfect subject!"

The needle started to register. When it was dead on the halfway mark, Brains took his hand off the control knob.

"Fire away," he said to McGurk.

McGurk glanced at the list.

"What is your name?"

"Béla Egri."

Needle steady. The truth.

"Where are you staying?"

"With Dad's Aunt Gerda. Mrs. Kranz."

Needle steady. The truth.

"Are you really a werefrog?"

The smile broadened, but there was no hesitation.

"Yes."

The needle flickered very slightly. Brains nodded at McGurk. It looked like it had been a lie. A cool lie, but a lie even so.

McGurk nodded back, then went on to the next question.

"But didn't you tell us there were no such things as werewolves and vampires?"

"Yes."

Needle steady. The truth.

"It was just that you didn't ask about *werefrogs*," Béla added.

"Oh, gosh! I *knew*—"

"Shut up, Willie. . . ." McGurk was thinking hard, I could tell. He'd come to the end of the prepared questions and I was beginning to wonder how he'd make out. Then he found a new one. "So if you are a werefrog, Béla, what is your favorite food?"

Without any hesitation, the boy said:

"Live flies and other bugs when I can get them. Also tubifex worms from the pet store. And sometimes cockroaches."

There was only the very slightest of flickers. If it was a lie, it was the coolest yet. McGurk raised his eyebrows. Brains frowned thoughtfully. Wanda made a face at the mention of worms. Willie shuddered.

I was too busy watching McGurk to have any feelings of my own. Under those raised eyebrows that gleam had suddenly appeared—clear and strong. I wondered. . . .

McGurk then asked:

"Are you going to turn into a frog again, Béla?"
This time there was a pause. Béla shrugged.

"Maybe," he said. "I don't know."

Not a flicker. The needle stayed dead center.
The truth.

Then, with the gleam brightening, McGurk said:

"What kind of a frog is it that you change into?
Some kind of Hungarian frog?"

And, once more without any hesitation, Béla said:

"*No! A Cuban tree frog!*"

Again only the very faintest of flickers. It was
either the truth or another extremely cool lie.

The gleam in McGurk's eyes had turned to a
glow.

"Well how about *that?*" he murmured. "A Cuban tree frog, huh? . . . O.K., kid—you can go back
to your suitcase now."

Béla frowned.

"But I like this place! Can't I stay and play with
you?"

"This isn't play. We have work to do. Officer
Grieg—see he gets home safely."

"But—" Béla looked ready to cry. Then: "Oh, all
right!" he yelled. "You wait! Just for that I *will*
change into a frog tonight! You'll see!"

And as Wanda escorted him to the door, he turned and made his snarly frog croak.

"Wow!" said Willie. "What did you go and get him mad for? He *meant* that, you know!"

McGurk was grinning slyly himself now.

"I hope he did. I really hope he did."

Then he turned to Brains.

"O.K., Officer Bellingham. I believe you now. If he's a werefrog I'm a werepotato. So tonight we run another test. One of *my* kind of tests. And if it works we'll have the case all sewed up."

Brains stared.

"A *scientific* test?"

"Very."

"What sort of equipment do you need?"

"Leave that to me. It's just a hunch so far, and I don't want to jinx everything by naming it. Just be sure to bring your tape recorder along tonight, Brains—that's all."

"Tape recorder?"

"Yeah. For the confession." McGurk got up from the rocking chair. "Now if you guys'll excuse me, I have some private inquiries to make. And keep your fingers crossed while I'm away. . . . O.K.? . . . Everything depends on this!"

8 Joey's Special Mission

McGurk gets very mysterious himself when he's working on one of his hunches. I guess it's because he's so proud and hates to look dumb if his ideas don't work out. But although it's understandable, it can be very maddening sometimes.

Like during the rest of that day, for instance.

He made two long visits downtown. I saw him coming home for lunch after the first of these and he was looking a bit anxious. When I asked him if his hunch wasn't working out after all, he forced a grin to his face and said: "Just a temporary hitch. Don't worry. Everything will be just fine by tonight."

Then he thought for a few seconds and suddenly put his hand on my shoulder.

"Come to think of it, Joey, you might just be able to help me with this."

I looked at him suspiciously.

For him to be letting me in so early on one of his special secrets meant only two things.

One—he hadn't a chance of succeeding by himself.

And two—the work required very high intelligence, probably involving writing a letter or something.

"How about Brains?" I said. "Shall we bring him in on it, too?"

He shook his head firmly.

"No!"

"But you said this was a *scientific* plan."

"It is. In a way. But it requires—uh—some very special talking."

"Talking? Not writing, then?"

"No—but talking that *sounds* like writing. Very smooth and respectable and—and responsible. Kind of."

I felt pleased. This sounded just my thing.

"Tell me about it," I said.

So he did. Up to a point.

He'd been spending the morning trying to find out about frogs—especially Cuban tree frogs.

"Where?"

"At the Town Museum—where else? I remembered Brains saying they'd once had an exhibition of stuffed frogs there. Here, take a look at this."

He pulled out a folded piece of paper. It was a Xerox copy of a museum exhibit description card. Here it is:

```
#38 A male CUBAN TREE FROG.  Cuban tree frogs
are natives of the West Indies, as their name
suggests, but they are also to be found in
Florida and Puerto Rico.  Note the toe disks,
typical of all tree frogs.  (See exhibits #39,
#40 and #41.)  They feed mainly at night,
when they often lurk around lighted windows,
which attract winged insects.  During the day
they hide in moist, dark places.  The voice of
the Cuban tree frog is a very loud, snarly rasp.
```

"Hey! That fits *our* frog!" I said. "That's the one we saw and heard—isn't it?"

The doubt came into my voice as I caught McGurk's expression. His own look of triumph had faded.

"Oh, sure!" he said. "That's *it*, all right. I even got to see a stuffed one—part of the collection they used to have on display there." He growled. The sound came out a bit snarly and rasping itself. "You'd think they'd be glad to lend a guy something like that, wouldn't you? Instead of leaving it gathering dust in the back of some old closet!"

I stared at him.

"You mean you asked to *borrow* it?"

He nodded.

"But why?" I asked.

The gleam came back in his eyes for a moment.

"For my plan."

"What *is* the plan?"

"I'll let you know on one condition, Joey. If you hurry up over lunch, put your best suit on, and come back and talk that guy into lending it to us. *Then* I'll tell you my plan." He paused and put a hand on my shoulder again. "If anyone can do it, you can," he added.

I knew what he meant. The Town Museum is part of the Town Library Center—which includes an art gallery and a music room. And while McGurk tends to get frowned on by the people down there—mainly because he will *not* learn to keep his voice down—I'm always welcome. I mean, for one thing, I've been a steady borrower of books since I was six. And for another, my father is a member of an organization called Friends of the Town Library Center. So our whole family is entitled to special privileges.

But—borrowing museum *exhibits?*

I tried to tell McGurk of my doubts, on the way down, that afternoon.

"The privileges mean getting tickets for special talks or shows—that kind of thing. It doesn't mean—"

"Sure! Sure! But they *know* you, Joey. They *trust* you. Just ask nice and polite and say it's for special research work."

"Special *research* work? And what if they ask for details? What do I tell them then, when *you* won't even let me know?"

"You'll think of something."

"Well, I'm not going to lie."

"You won't have to. When *you* say you want it for something like that, you won't have to go into details. Now take off that dumb hat and smooth down your hair and put your glasses straight. We're nearly there."

Well, I was still very doubtful as we climbed the stairs to the museum. I hated to disappoint McGurk and I was dying to know what his plan was, but I didn't give much for our chances.

"You sure I shouldn't do this alone?" I said, when we'd crossed the floor of the main room, past all the model dinosaur exhibits, and were standing outside a door marked G. E. EVANS, CURATOR.

McGurk hesitated, then nodded.

"Good thinking, Joey. I'll pretend I'm not with you."

Then, while I knocked nervously, he went and lurked behind the glass case containing the skull of a dinosaur.

The door opened.

"Yes? . . . Oh—hi, Joey!"

I blinked. It wasn't the man I knew as the curator. It wasn't a man at all. It was Joanne Cooper, the girl whose valuable engagement ring we helped to find in the Case of the Great Rabbit Rip-off.

"Hi, McGurk!" she said, looking over my head.

But when McGurk lurks, he really lurks. He ducked farther behind the skull so that all we could see was a patch of red hair and a glint of green through one of the eye sockets.

Joanne shrugged.

"What's with *him?* Don't tell me he's gotten shy. Or—hey—is he on another case?"

"Well, sort of," I said. "Have you seen Mr. Evans anywhere around, Joanne?"

"He's out this afternoon," she said. "I'm in charge.

Is there something I can do?"

I stared at her.

"You? I—uh—*you?* You *work* here?"

It wasn't the smooth writing-type talking Mc-Gurk had expected of me, I know. But I'd been taken by surprise. And I was also getting excited. All at once, our prospects of a frog loan had brightened 100 percent.

"Yes," she was saying. "I'm Mr. Evans's secretary. I work here part-time—afternoons mostly. Ever since the beginning of last week. I may not know everything about everything in here, but you can always try me."

I took a big breath.

"Joanne," I said, "do you know what happened to that old collection of stuffed frogs?"

"Sure," she said. "They're all piled up in a closet in the storeroom. Junk mostly." She frowned. "Funny you should ask," she said. "Mr. Evans tells me someone was in here this morning, asking to *borrow* one." She laughed. "Can you imagine anyone wanting to borrow something like that?"

"Yeah!" said McGurk. "Me!"

He'd come out of hiding. His eyes were shining now.

"Oh-oh!" said Joanne. "So that's what this visit is all about, is it? Well, let me tell you guys, if it was up to me you could borrow the whole collection."

"We'd bring it straight back tomorrow morning," said McGurk. "Promise!"

"And it *is* for special scientific research," I said. "A really careful study—"

Joanne was still shaking her head. All my fine words were having no effect.

But McGurk's eyes had a very determined gleam in them—a gleam almost as bright as the ring she was wearing. And he was now staring at that ring very closely—so closely I thought he'd touch it with his nose.

"I see you still have the ring, Joanne," he said, softly.

And that did it. Where all my fine long words had failed, those few soft short ones of his worked like a charm.

She flushed slightly, sighed, shrugged, then smiled.

"Oh, well!" she said. "So long as you promise to take care of the frog. And bring it back in the afternoon, direct to me. . . . Come on. Show me which one it was."

The Surprise Package

9

McGurk got me very mad on the way home when he refused to tell me exactly what he wanted the frog for.

"I haven't worked out all the fine details yet," he said.

"But you *promised!*"

"Only if you managed to talk the museum people into lending it to us," he said. "Which you didn't. *I* did."

"But—"

"Don't worry, Joey. You'll find out. Tonight, at Mrs. Kranz's."

So I was just as furious as the others when he

showed up that night with a bulge in his pocket and a great fat smug smile on his face and he *still* refused to tell us about it.

"Later," he said. "Wait until Mrs. Kranz has gone into the garage and the kid's settled down."

And that was how it had to be.

"All right!" said Wanda, the second Mrs. Kranz had closed the kitchen door and gone off into the dusk, back to her statue. "Now you tell us, McGurk, or I turn in my ID card! This is supposed to be a team, remember!"

"Yes," said Brains. "I carried out my part of the instructions." He patted the small tape recorder he'd placed on a side table. "Now you keep your promise or this recorder stays in its case."

"Sure!" said McGurk. "Only keep your voices down. I want to hear it the minute that kid makes a move."

This time we hadn't bothered fixing the microphone in the bedroom, so we'd left the living-room door open instead.

We got quiet, not so much to be able to hear Béla as to encourage McGurk to get on with his explanation.

"Well," he said, at last, "I spent a very interesting morning—doing some scientific research."

"Oh?" said Brains. "On what?"

"On frogs," said McGurk. "I've been finding out about Cuban tree frogs, and I know for sure now that the frog up there *is* one of that kind."

Note that. "*I've*" been finding out. And "*I*" know for sure now. Not a word about *me*.

Brains sniffed.

"Is that all? I could have told you that. I could have looked it up in my encyclopedia and—"

"What *I* was doing was better than looking in some old encyclopedia," said McGurk. "I went straight to the Town Museum. Doing my research with the *experts*."

Brains's mouth sagged open. He began to look at McGurk with new respect. So did the others.

"Go on, McGurk!" said Wanda. "So what did you find?"

"This!" said McGurk. "For one thing."

And he produced the slip of paper with details about the frog.

Wanda, Willie, and Brains crowded around to read it.

"Is that *all?*" said Brains again. "There isn't a

word in there I couldn't have got out of my encyclopedia."

McGurk was leering at us. He was getting nauseating again. He must have seen the look in my eyes, because he went on quickly:

"Forget about your encyclopedia, Brains. *Think* about some of those details. Because they just may clinch the whole case. Especially the detail about how Cuban tree frogs like to feed at night at lighted windows."

"Oh?" said Wanda. "You mean—?"

"I mean, like that *very* brightly lighted window up there," said McGurk. "They—" He stopped. "Listen!"

It wasn't a croak. Just a faint creak. It could have been a floorboard, or a door hinge, or a stiff drawer.

"I think the show is just about to begin," whispered McGurk. "Keep quiet and follow me."

Then he led us out into the front yard, which was quite dark by this time, apart from the window near the top of the tree.

"You think the frog is in the tree now, McGurk?" I asked.

He shook his head.

"Just watch—and don't make a sound."

Well, for a few minutes we didn't make a sound. All we could hear was the faint tapping of Mrs. Kranz's hammer from around the side of the house. Then Wanda suddenly caught her breath and said:

"Look!"

A shadow had appeared at the window. Then it became more solid: the silhouette of Béla's head and shoulders.

"What's he doing?" whispered Willie. "Is *he* going into the tree?"

But Béla had opened the bottom of the window only a few inches wider than we'd left it. Then we saw him fumble about and we heard his nails scraping on the frame of the screen. Then that too was opened—but just a crack.

"The frog's dining room," said McGurk. "Béla's just opened the serving hatch. See!"

Béla had stepped back, but there still remained one small dark shape, about the size of his fist, that began to make slight movements on its own. The bugs had started to fly in through the crack.

"Now," said McGurk, "we go back in—"

"And nail the frog?" asked Brains.

"And *wait!*" said McGurk, sternly. "Wait until

it's had a good feed and Béla decides to pull his big werefrog act again, like he threatened this morning."

"But I don't get it," said Willie, once we were back in the living room. "Why don't we catch it while it's busy eating? With its back to us?"

"We wouldn't stand a chance. One leap and it would be out in the tree and Béla would be laughing his head off." McGurk looked about to do the same himself at that moment. I've never seen him look so pleased. "No," he said, slowly taking a package from his pocket. "We're going to teach that kid a lesson he'll never forget. With this."

Then he opened the small box and it is truly a wonder its contents didn't blow away, the way those other three all gasped together.

"Hey—where did you get *that*, McGurk?" asked Brains in a croaky voice, as he stared at the replica of the frog upstairs: a slightly battered, rather dusty, but very lifelike stuffed Cuban tree frog.

"From the museum—where else?" said McGurk gleefully. "And it took some heavy talking and promising to get them to loan it to the Organization, believe me. But the question you *should* have asked is what am I going to do with it? Right? . . . So if you'll just come a little closer, and keep your voices down, I'll tell you. . . ."

Well, even for McGurk, that idea was a winner, and no kidding. I mean, it was so beautiful I forgave him on the spot and we nearly choked trying to keep ourselves from cheering out loud as he revealed it to us, step by step.

10 The Slaying of the Monster

We could hardly wait for the croaking after that, even though McGurk had us all hard at work in a corner away from the door, quietly rehearsing what we had to say and do. Brains was especially impatient. He kept breaking off to listen and cluck and say, "I wish we'd fixed the microphone up again!" But McGurk told him not to worry.

"We'll hear it all right, same as we did the first night. I want you to concentrate on your tape recorder this time."

And our crime-lab expert was just starting to complain again, when the sound came rasping down the stairs and through the door:

"*Shushnaquaaaraaaaarnaaaragraaark!*"

Not as loud as through the amplifier, of course—but unmistakable.

"Right, men!" McGurk muttered, leading us out into the hallway, in time for a second snarling croak. "Remember what I told you." Then in a loud voice he said: "*There! What did I tell you? He's changed into a frog again!*"

"Oh, gosh!" said Wanda, also out loud. "I—I'm scared!"

"Me, too!" I cried out. "Let's—let's just drop the whole thing, McGurk. We can't tangle with a were-frog!"

By now we'd reached the top of the stairs. McGurk nodded to Brains. Brains nodded back, then said, over the top of another long rasping croak from the room: "There's no such things as—as werefrogs!"

But this time he said it the way McGurk had told him to: in a shaky voice, full of doubt.

Then it was Willie's turn.

"Oh!-oh! I-smell-the-swamp-smell-again! I-am-getting-out-of-here!"

It came out very hammy. I hoped it wouldn't give our plan away. McGurk glared at Willie. I thought it was because he'd been thinking the same thing. I mean, Willie's acting really did stink. But no. I soon realized it was all part of McGurk's act. He was putting everything he had into playing his own part—and McGurk is some actor even when he's not trying.

"*Stay where you are, Officer Sandowsky!*" he roared. "*Stay where you are, all of you! That thing in there is an evil monster. It has captured the soul of Béla!*"

Then he flung open the door, cried, "Leave it to me, men!"—and marched up to the bed.

Well, at first it was the werefrog scene all over again. No sign of Béla. Only the frog, leering at us in a seemingly friendly fashion from the pillow.

But this time, instead of running, we clustered around the bed. Then McGurk yelled, "Gotcha!" and brought his fists down with a terrible thump, about two feet away from the frog.

He'd missed it intentionally, of course. And, also intentionally, I made a quieter grab at the frog, meaning to whisk it out of sight under the covers.

The trouble was, the frog hadn't been in on the rehearsal. It certainly wasn't *my* fault. In fact if it was anybody's fault, it was McGurk's for thumping down so hard, because it scared that frog so much it leaped high in the air, seconds before my clutching fingers had reached the pillow. Then it went hurtling past Willie's nose.

The flight of the frog caused Willie to give a yell of fright that really was genuine, and even Wanda gave a little scream. But she remembered her lines and the show went on as planned when she said, "Oh, McGurk! You've killed it!"

"*Yeah!*" growled McGurk, after giving me a dirty look and glancing around to make sure that the real frog was out of sight after all. "*That's the last croak this werefrog will ever give!*"

And that did it. Suddenly the closet door burst open and a small sobbing blur of a boy in yellow pajamas came dashing toward the bed.

"Oh, no! Oh, no! You haven't—you can't have—"

Then: *"Murderers!"* he yelled, pulling up dead at the sight of the stiff little browny-green body on the bed, next to McGurk's hand. "You killed him! You killed Fidel! My best friend! *Fidel!"*

And when his groping fingers touched the stiff little legs, he was so shocked he just broke down and his tears began to gush over the body he was gently cradling in his hands. I mean really gush, because by this time the body was upside down and the tears must have blinded him to the label pasted there:

CUBAN TREE FROG

(Hyla septentrionalis)

Adult male

"Hey—*McGurk!"* Wanda murmured huskily.

She looked all set to cry herself.

I knew how she felt. I was beginning to feel like a heel, too, and I'm sure Willie and Brains were. Even McGurk had started to get red, and his smile of triumph had taken a sharp dip.

"It's all right, Béla!" he muttered. "It—"

"Murderer!" growled Béla, jerking his shaking

shoulders away from McGurk's arm. "You killed the only—"

Then the real frog, the phantom frog, the *former* phantom frog, Fidel, spoke up.

"*Shnaquaaark!*" he rasped, from somewhere above our heads and behind us.

We turned. He was perched on the top edge of a picture of George Washington on the wall, the little bubble-gum piece of skin under his mouth beginning to swell up ready for another comment.

"*Fidel!*" cried Béla. He was staring up through his tears, as if he couldn't believe it. Then he glanced down at the body in his hands and must have noticed the label for the first time. With a yelp of pure joy, he tossed the stuffed frog back onto the bed and pushed his way through us to the picture. "Fidel! They didn't kill you after all!"

"Of course not!" said McGurk, gruffly, watching the frog hop down onto Béla's hand and then climb across onto the boy's shoulder, where he stayed clinging for the rest of the interview. "What do you take us for?"

"I'm sorry," said Béla. "But—I thought—"

"Forget it," said McGurk, glancing across to make sure that Brains had the recorder running and the microphone handy. "So *now* would you like to tell us about the frog?"

Béla nodded. He brushed a wet cheek against Fidel's nose and said, "Oh, all right! I guess I'd better—huh, Fidel?"

And Fidel gave a soft croak that must have signified yes, because that's when we got the full confession.

11 The Confession

I sometimes think there might be quite a lot of truth in McGurk's earlier werefrog theory, after all. I don't mean that it's possible for a person to change into a creature and back again. No. But I'm beginning to think that sometimes a person and a creature can be such good friends that they're just not *complete* without each other. Like Béla and Fidel. Without the frog on his shoulder or in his hands or at least in sight, Béla was a sly, bratty, bad-tempered kid. But with Fidel there beside him, openly, he was totally different: friendly, relaxed, a real nice regular little guy. Even during the confession it began to show through.

"I got him last year in Florida," he began. "He was just a baby then and I've looked after him ever since. My dad said he bet I'd soon get tired of him, but no way—huh, Fidel? I clean his tank, I catch flies for him, I buy his worms—"

"Excuse me," said Wanda. "You're talking about when you're all back home, right? I mean not *here*, with Mrs. Kranz?"

"Ah, yeah!" Béla sighed. "She doesn't like frogs, you know. When I went to see Mom in the hospital, the first day, Mom told me that. She said I mustn't bring Fidel here. She said I'd have to take Fidel to the pet store and have them board him there. And I said I would, but—"

He shrugged, and Fidel gave a gentle snarl at the very idea.

"You decided to bring him with you as a kind of stowaway, right?" said McGurk.

"Right. I knew he'd probably make a noise at night. But I hoped she'd be too scared to look too carefully, especially when I pretended not to hear it."

"Good thinking!" said McGurk, nodding respectfully. "For a kid. . . . But you didn't count on her hiring a detective organization like us, did you?"

This was the point where McGurk usually gets obnoxious. But he still spoke quietly, more in sympathy than in triumph.

"No," said the boy. "Before you stuck your noses —I mean, before you were hired—it was easy. I hid Fidel in the bathroom during the day, on some soaking wet towels in back of an old cupboard behind the tub. Then when he woke up, when it got dark outside, I'd bring him in here."

"To feed at the window?"

"Yes. The tree out there is full of all kinds of bugs and—"

"And as soon as the light shines they're all stirred up, right?"

"Hey! Right!" Now it was Béla's turn to look respectfully at McGurk. "I'll let you see him eat some more flies if you like. It makes his eyes sink down into his skull and—"

"Not now, son. You just go on telling us what happened. I mean the first night, when we came in looking for him. Where was he then?"

Béla grinned.

"In the suitcase. I was always ready to use it as a quick hiding place if Aunty Kranz came in. Either there or out on the tree itself. I sometimes let him

go out there for a special treat. He'd always come back in when I called." Béla frowned. "But I was worried some sudden noise might scare him out there. So it was mainly the suitcase in emergencies." He grinned again. "I was glad you didn't have your search warrant that first night, though."

"And the second night?"

"Oh, *then*, *that* time, I meant to hide him in the bathroom—"

"After you'd deliberately let him croak into the microphone?" said Brains.

"Yeah! I thought it would be fun. But he slipped out of my hands onto the bed, and you were already coming up the stairs. So *I* was the one who hid in the bathroom. Then later, after you'd run away and you came back upstairs again, we switched places—Fidel in the bathroom and me in bed."

"But we searched the bathroom that time!" said McGurk.

"Yes," said Béla, "but you were looking for *me*, a boy—not a frog in a little space."

Béla started to laugh.

"Oh, but it was funny! Eh, Fidel? When you all came in and—heh! heh!—thought we were a—heh! heh!—*werefrog!*"

McGurk grunted.

"So *that's* where you got the idea from!"

"Yeah! Heh! heh! From *you!* From you yourself!"

Then all at once Béla's laughter faded. Maybe it was the look on McGurk's face.

"But, hey—we're friends, right? I mean—" He looked around and his eyes flashed desperately. "I mean, you're not going to give us away, me and Fidel, to Aunty Kranz, are you?"

"Of course not!" said Wanda. "What makes you think we'd do a thing like that?"

"Hold it, Officer Grieg!" McGurk gave Wanda a stern look. "Mrs. Kranz hired us to solve a mystery, remember. She's paying us a good fee—"

"Well, she can keep the fee then!" said Wanda

"—and it's our duty!" McGurk growled. "Our duty toward our client!"

There was no arguing with that. I mean, either you do a thing like this right or you forget it and go play cops and robbers.

"I agree, McGurk," I said. "Only it does seem pretty tough. . . ."

"Yeah!" said Willie. "Why don't we just show her the stuffed frog and say it's the real one and we killed it?"

All this time, the four brown eyes of Béla and Fidel were watching us—and I could swear Fidel's were just as much pleading as Béla's.

"What we *could* do," said Wanda, "is look after Fidel for you, until your mom and dad get well enough to go home again. I mean, I'd be only too glad to have him at our house and look after him like he was my own." She gave a little laugh. "You know, *I'm* a tree-climber, too. And—and you'd be welcome to stop by any time and spend as long as you like."

But Béla was shaking his head, the tears starting again.

"He'd pine away—he'd—"

Then we heard the door downstairs.

"Gosh! It's nine already!" said Wanda. "It's Mrs. Kranz!"

Which is when McGurk took charge again.

"Right!" he said. "Leave this to me. Béla—hide the frog and get into bed. Brains—have that recorder ready to play back the minute I ask you to. . . . O.K.?"

Béla was already on his way into the bathroom. His faith in McGurk was quite touching. But as we went down to face Mrs. Kranz, I only hoped our leader knew what he was doing.

12 The Twenty-Five Dollar Solution

I needn't have worried. McGurk handled it perfectly. He told us afterward that it came to him in a flash—after hearing Wanda's suggestion.

"But first we had to play that confession back to Mrs. Kranz and count on it melting her heart the way it had melted some of *yours*," he said.

Well, it did just that. I mean, at first Mrs. Kranz's eyes bulged pretty hard when she learned that her nephew's kid had been harboring an exotic tree frog in the house—but before long those eyes had begun to brim with tears.

"Oh, dear!" she said, with tears spilling over and making streaks in the stone dust on her face.

"Poor little boy! I suspected all along that the noise might have had something to do with Béla. That's really why I hired *you*—to find out for sure—instead of calling in the exterminators. But I'd no idea anyone could get so attached to a—a frog."

"Why don't you let him show it to you, Mrs. Kranz?" said Wanda. "Fidel is so cute—"

"Officer Grieg!"

McGurk glared at her, and no wonder. The mere thought of seeing the frog face to face had set Mrs. Kranz shaking.

"The trouble is, Mrs. Kranz," he said, "if you make Béla part with Fidel it could—well—you heard him on the tape. It could wreck Béla's health." He frowned, looking very official. "And that could get you into real trouble with the law!"

"I know!" said Mrs. Kranz, miserably. "But what else *can* I do? The thought of a frog loose in the house for a whole month. . . ."

She shuddered again.

And that's where McGurk pounced.

"Sure! But what if it *wasn't* loose? What if we made it a top-security den? Not just an old tank, but like a dog pen, with fine-mesh chicken wire, to go in the basement?"

"Well. . . ."

She was beginning to soften up.

"But it would have to have water!" a voice piped up from the doorway. "And—and the temperature would have to be controlled. And he'd need a tree of *some* kind. And fresh food. And—and. . . ."

It was Béla.

I was glad to see that he'd left the frog upstairs. Its presence might have blown everything at that stage.

"Sure!" McGurk said, taking it all in his stride, at

the very top of his form. "Why not? You could fix
a thermostat heater, couldn't you, Brains? And make
sure the pen was frogproof, yet big enough for
Béla to stand in it whenever he wanted?"

"No problem," said Brains. "But—"

"And I could get a bush from the abandoned
lot," said Wanda.

"And I'm a good carpenter," said Willie.

"And I could help with the food supply," I said,
already thinking of how I might use a lamp and a
jar to trap flies and moths.

"*But*," said Brains, "it's going to cost a lot. Especially the electronics."

"What do you call a lot?" said McGurk.

"Well—I'd say around twenty-five dollars," said
Brains. "Give or take a dollar or two."

McGurk sighed with relief. His face broke up in a
big freckly grin.

"No problem," he said. "Mrs. Kranz already owes
us thirty dollars. Right, ma'am?"

Mrs. Kranz nodded. She started to say something
about meeting the cost herself. This could only
mean, of course, that she was willing to go along with
the idea, and that made McGurk so pleased that he
wouldn't hear of her paying a cent more.

"Being paid all that money for baby-sitting was a steal anyway," he said. "Even when the baby-sitting was only a cover."

And we all agreed—proud of our leader's generous spirit.

But then Generous Jack McGurk had to go and spoil it with his next remark.

"By the way, kid," he said, turning to the over-joyed Béla. "Was that *really* Hungarian, what you said to me the other day?"

"Sure!" said Béla—and he repeated them again: those strange words that I'd mistaken for the Curse of the Werefrogs.

"What does it mean?" asked McGurk.

"Well—" Béla hesitated, then shrugged and, this time grinning shyly rather than slyly, said: "You will never find the frog!"

McGurk smirked. He even had the gall to say:

"That's what I thought it meant!"

Then he topped it all off by adding in his most obnoxious manner:

"But that was before you realized who you were dealing with, right? So tell me this. What's Hungarian for: '*I shoulda known better than to think I could outsmart Jack P. McGurk*'?"

We looked at each other.

Jack P. McGurk!

No mention of the Organization!

Wanda turned to Béla.

"Better make that Hungarian for '*Jack P. McGurk's a lot like a frog himself.*'"

"Oh, yeah?" said McGurk, glaring at her.

"Yeah!" said Wanda, glaring back. "He's got a great big mouth and he's always shooting it off!"

Then everyone broke up laughing—including McGurk and even Mrs. Kranz—when, faintly from upstairs, there came a croak of what sounded like full agreement from Fidel, the Phantom Frog.